P9-DDF-657

TRICK of the TALE

For Wil and Cait
J. & C. M.

To Hana and Matej, my own little tricksters
T. T.

Text copyright © 2008 by John and Caitlín Matthews
Illustrations copyright © 2008 by Tomislav Tomić

First U.S. edition 2008

Library of Congress Cataloging-in-Publication Data is available.

Library of Congress Catalog Card Number pending

ISBN 978-0-7636-3646-3

2 4 6 8 10 9 7 5 3 1

Printed in China

This book was set in Quercus Regular.
The illustrations were done in ink with watercolor.

Candlewick Press
2067 Massachusetts Avenue
Cambridge, Massachusetts 02140

visit us at www.candlewick.com

TRICK of the TALE

A COLLECTION OF TRICKSTER TALES

JOHN & CAITLÍN MATTHEWS

ILLUSTRATED BY
TOMISLAV TOMIĆ

CANDLEWICK PRESS
CAMBRIDGE, MASSACHUSETTS

CONTENTS

INTRODUCTION

The oldest teachers of human beings are the animals, and none are more clever or venerable instructors than the tricksters.

Throughout world culture, tricksters such as Hare and Raven are honored for playing important roles in the creation of the earth. Their bluffs and schemes taught skills without which we human beings would be poor, helpless animals indeed. The earliest storytellers had nothing but admiration for the trickster animals, who showed people how to live with zest and cunning. Our ancestors even drew such animals on the walls of their caves thousands of years ago.

These tales are told around the world—in Asia, Africa, Europe, and the Americas—in cultures whose storytelling traditions had no knowledge of one another but which somehow all have the adventures of tricksters in common. We can also trace some of the ways in which the trickster tradition has traveled across the globe. Survivors of the terrible Middle Passage from Africa to America, for example, brought trickster stories with them, including those featuring the daring tricks of Ananse—stories full of humor and wisdom that helped them to triumph over adversity. These stories also began the African-American storytelling tradition, which produced new tricksters such as Brer Rabbit.

The appeal of the trickster is simple—whether hungry wolf or helpless frog, the trickster finds a way to win out when all seems hopeless. Whatever its size, each trickster animal draws upon its own intelligence, abilities, and cunning resilience to bluff, cheat, dodge, or decoy—and so to escape from present danger and gain its freedom. Whether you are a clever fox or an underdog, these tales show you how to value life's gifts to the fullest.

We hope you enjoy these stories, for each has a special trick in the tale.

A HILL of BEANS

Hare is a favorite trickster in Japanese mythology.
Here he plays a trick on his own friends.

One sunny morning, Hare, Otter, Monkey, and Badger were out and about, looking for trouble, when they saw a man with a heavy sack walking along the road.

"Let's play a trick on that peddler," said Hare.

"What shall we do?" asked Badger.

"Watch this!" said Hare, and he raced off in a cloud of dust.

He jumped out in front of the peddler and danced for him, hitting the ground with his big hind feet and jumping around like a clown. The peddler, deciding to catch this amazing animal, put down his sack and raced after the hare. But as he ran around the corner, the wily creature sped off so quickly that the trees bent over as he passed. Before the peddler could return to his sack, Hare's three friends grabbed it and dragged it away.

Later they met to view the spoils and decide how to divide them. When they emptied the sack, they found a block of salt, a woven mat, a little waterwheel, and a big bag of beans. Hare, as usual, had the most to say.

"I know how we should divide these things," he said. "Otter, you live in the water and love crabs. You should have the salt, because salted crab is really tasty."

"Agreed," said Otter, looking pleased.

"And Monkey, you should have the mat," said Hare. "You sleep on bare rocks and branches all the time. The mat will make you much more comfortable."

"Agreed," said Monkey, smiling.

"And as for you, dear Badger," Hare said, "you should have the waterwheel, because it will whirl and twirl in the entrance to your den and be most entertaining."

"Agreed," said Badger happily.

"That just leaves the beans for me," said Hare, looking gloomy. "Oh, well, I suppose I can make do with them."

Otter went back to the river with the block of salt and dropped it into the water. But before he found a single crab to eat, it had melted away.

Monkey took the woven mat and laid it out carefully on a rock. Then he curled up and tried to go to sleep. But every time he nodded off, the mat slipped off the rock and Monkey woke up with a shock on the hard ground.

And Badger—well, he took the waterwheel and placed it at the entrance to his den. Then he lay down and watched and watched and waited for it to turn. But, of course, with no water, it stayed completely still.

All three animals realized that they had been tricked by Hare. Hopping mad, they marched off to find their old friend.

By this time, Hare had eaten all the beans until he couldn't manage another one. But he kept thinking, *My friends are going to be angry with me, and pretty soon they'll come this way.*

Finally Hare came up with a clever plan. He took the leftover bean skins and stuck them all over his fat stomach.

Soon after, Otter, Monkey, and Badger came marching along, looking very fierce. Hare lay down on the ground and began to groan.

"Oooh! Oooh! My poor stomach! I wish I hadn't eaten all those beans. Look, they are bursting out of me!"

The animals saw the bean skins all over Hare's stomach and thought he must be in terrible pain.

"Well, we *were* really angry," they said. "But now that we see that you had the worst of it, we're sorry instead."

And they all went off home—leaving Hare rolling on the ground and laughing till he almost burst.

BRER RABBIT and the FATAL IMITATION

Brer Rabbit is a favorite character in African-American storytelling.

Every day on his way to work, Brer Rabbit saw big old Rooster sitting on top of the barn, crowing. And every night when he came home again, there was the shrewd bird, sitting in the same spot, but without a head and with only one leg.

"Hey, Mr. Rooster," yelled Brer Rabbit one morning, "why do you cut off your head and foot every night and put them back on again in the morning?"

Rooster opened one yellow eye. "That's how I get my rest," he said.

"What a fine idea," said Brer Rabbit, thinking how wise old Rooster was.

So when he went home that night, he told his wife to cut off his head and three of his legs so that he could get a really good night's sleep.

But when the knife touched his front leg, Brer Rabbit screamed so loudly that he woke old Rooster up.

Rooster took his head out from under his wing, where he had been shading his eyes from the moonlight, and he unfolded his leg, which he had tucked under himself to keep warm.

"Brer Rabbit, stop that noise!" he shouted.

So Brer Rabbit nursed his sore leg and didn't try that trick again.

How Raven
Stole Back the Light

This tale, from the Inuit people of Canada,
shows how a trickster could sometimes be helpful to mankind.

When the world began, everyone lived on this side of the sky. But a great magician named Tupalik was curious and decided to find out what lay on the other side. He cut a hole in the sky and climbed through. Tupalik liked what he found so much that he decided to build a house there and take up residence with his family.

But Tupalik's wife did not like her new home. It was always dark and cold on the other side of the sky, and she missed her friends and felt lonely. So Tupalik decided to cheer her up by bringing her the light. He climbed through the hole in the sky, grabbed the sun and moon, and thrust them into two bags. Then he returned home and hung the bags from the roof of their house.

After that, Tupalik let the light out only when he wanted to, on his side of the sky, and the rest of the world spent their days in darkness.

Soon everyone on this side of the sky grew thin and pale from lack of light, so they went in search of Raven, who had helped them before.

"Raven," they cried, "someone has stolen the moon and the sun. We are dying from lack of light! Please, please, can you get it back for us?"

Raven thought hard. "I'm sure Tupalik has something to do with this," he said. He flew across the world until he saw the hole in the sky and went through it. He found Tupalik dozing in the warmth of the sun, which he happened to have let out that day.

"Hey, Tupalik," said Raven, "I want the sun and moon back."

But Tupalik laughed and shook his head. "Go away, little raven. I need the sun and moon to cheer up my wife. Besides, I like them too much to let them go."

Raven flew off, thinking of ways to steal back the sun and moon. Then he saw a beautiful maiden going to fetch water from the river. Raven knew she must be Tupalik's daughter. An idea flashed into his head, and with a chuckle he flew down to the river's edge and turned himself into a tiny feather floating on the water.

Filling her jug in the stream, Tupalik's daughter didn't notice when the feather floated inside. She didn't notice when, taking a huge gulp of water, the feather slipped down her throat. A few months later, she gave birth to a beautiful baby boy, who was really still Raven in disguise.

Tupalik and his wife were delighted by their grandson, not knowing he was actually Raven. They doted on the baby, giving him everything he asked for. And Raven made sure that he was always asking for something—yelling all day at the top of his lungs.

One day, while Tupalik was away hunting, Raven started crying for the bags that held the sun and moon. At first Tupalik's wife and daughter ignored the baby, but soon they grew so sick of hearing him wail and scream that they let him play with the bag that held the moon. When they weren't looking, Raven untied the bag, and the moon flew out and vanished through the smoke hole in the roof.

When Tupalik came home, he was furious, but at the sight of his grandson, smiling and peaceful, he softened. "After all, I still have the sun," he said.

Soon the old magician settled down to sleep, and at once, Raven began to scream and cry for the bag that held the sun. Tupalik, weary and wanting sleep, told his wife to give the baby anything as long as it kept him quiet.

So Tupalik's wife took down the bag and gave it to the baby. As soon as she was looking the other way, Raven ran outside and turned back into his own form. The bag was tied too tight for him to open, so Raven flew back through the hole in the sky, carrying the bag in his talons.

The moon was back on our side of the sky by this time, having floated through the hole Tupalik had made, and life had begun to get back to normal, though the people still missed the sun.

Flying across the moonlit sky, Raven grew tired and hungry. Spying some fishermen, he cried out, "Please give me some fish—I'll let out the sun if you do."

Now, Raven had been gone for so long that the people had forgotten about asking him to steal back the sun, so the fishermen were reluctant to give him anything. Raven pecked angrily at the bag, and a few bright spots of light flew out, becoming the stars.

"Maybe he does have the sun," the fishermen said, and they gave Raven some food.

As soon as he was strong enough, Raven tore open the bag and the sun flew out. At first, the light blinded everyone, but after a while, they grew used to it again and threw a huge party for Raven to thank him.

As for Tupalik and his family, some say that they moved back to this side of the sky. Others swear that they live on the other side to this day, and that every now and then Tupalik manages to steal back the sun. But clever Raven always manages to return it to us.

A Home
of One's Own

*The rivalry between Leopard and Sungura the Hare is told in this story
from the Swahili-speaking people of Africa.*

Long ago, when all the animals lived together on the plains of Africa, there were two
creatures who had no home of their own. One of these was Sungura the Hare. Being
small, he was in constant danger of being trampled on or eaten by the larger animals.

"Small I am, but swift I am," he said. "The bush is no place for me. I must find the
perfect place to build my house, and then I can seek a wife and raise a family in peace."

So he took himself to the highest hill and found a grassy clearing. With his powerful
back feet, he danced in a joyful circle to mark out the place to build his hut. Then he
scampered down the south side of the hill to fetch sticks to make a frame for his house.

Now, there was another creature who wanted his own house. Leopard was greedy
and bad-tempered. No one wanted to share a house with him because he was such a
bully. Aloof and alone, he growled into the dusk, "Sad I am, but fierce I am. I will find a
place where I can see my food coming, and there I will build my house." He found the
highest hill and saw a perfect circle already marked in a grassy clearing. Leopard slunk
down the north side of the hill to find sticks for the frame of his house.

Sungura returned to the circle first and piled up his sticks. Then he rushed down
to the forest looking for vines to tie the sticks together. As Sungura scampered down the
hill, Leopard returned with his sticks and saw a pile already lying there. "What good
fortune! I wonder who dropped these here. Now I must find some mud." And away he
ran to the river.

Sungura returned and began to erect the sticks and tie them together. "Small I am, but swift I am to build the house where my family will live," he sang to himself. Then the hare ran downhill to bring reeds from the river to thatch the roof.

When Leopard returned with a gourd filled with river mud, he was mystified to see the hut beginning to take shape. He examined the neat way in which the sticks were tied together.

"Fierce I am, but glad I am," he purred, bowing his head. "Who else has done this work but my revered ancestors who roamed the bush before me? They must have looked upon my struggles and decided to help me build my house with their great power."

He began to splash the mud over the woven sticks to make the walls. Satisfied with his work, he too went to fetch reeds to thatch the roof.

Both Sungura and Leopard worked fast, each believing that it was his own revered ancestors who were helping with the work, until night fell and, between them, the hut was finished. The great red sun went down beyond the shimmering heat of the earth, and the dark cloak of night covered the bush. As the stars began to splash the darkness with points of light, both Hare and Leopard climbed the hill. Weary with work, each crawled into the hut and curled himself up in the darkness, neither one noticing the other.

Both slept deeply in the fragrant darkness, the deep sleep that has no dreams. But as the sun rose the next morning, a time when all the animals wake to seek water, Leopard snapped open both of his yellow eyes to see the hare Sungura in his house.

"Leave my house, little hare, or I shall have you for breakfast!" he snarled.

Sungura answered before he had time to be afraid: "But this house is mine! I built it yesterday with the help of my ancestors."

Leopard narrowed his yellow eyes. "You are wrong, Sungura. It was I who built this house yesterday, with the help of *my* ancestors."

Sungura suddenly understood and laughed. "I see the way of it.

We both built this house yesterday, turn and turn about. Our ancestors didn't help us at all—the leopard helped the hare and the hare helped the leopard. Since we have both done the work, I suggest that we both share this house."

Leopard drew himself up in a mighty stretch, ready to disagree, but the law of the animals was clear: whoever worked must receive the fruits of his or her labor.

"If we must share, then we need a wall between us," said Leopard.

And so Sungura and Leopard did their last piece of work together, erecting a wall of woven reeds, and then each went to his own side of the hut.

Now that Sungura had a house of his own, he raced down to the bush to ask the most beautiful female hare to marry him. Soon Sungura had both wife and children. Leopard became even more bad-tempered with a noisy family living on the other side of the flimsy wall. He swished his tail and raised his nose and tried to ignore them at first, but then his greed began to grow.

Sungura and his wife made a happy home for their children, but Sungura never forgot his neighbor's anger just beyond the thin wall. He lay sleepless many a night, working out a trick to protect his family from the leopard's appetite. With his wife's help, he planned what they should do.

One morning, Leopard was woken up by Sungura's children hollering. From beyond the wall came the clatter of dishes as Sungura's children played noisily.

"What a din!" he growled, covering his ears with his paws.

Leopard flexed his claws. It was time to get these noisy neighbors out of his house. It was breakfast time, after all. As he stretched, he heard Sungura ask his wife, "Why are our children so noisy and badly behaved this morning?"

Sungura's wife said loudly, "Oh, husband, they are hungry. The last of the elephant meat that you brought home is all eaten up. You will have to fetch some more."

Sungura's own voice came through the wall, "Oh, wife! Don't tell me I shall have to hunt more elephants! What a bore!"

"Elephant meat?" breathed Leopard, shocked to his spots. "How can a little hare hunt elephants? He must be more cunning than I realized." And for the rest of the day, Leopard was very quiet, so as not to disturb Sungura the Mighty Elephant Hunter.

But greed and laziness soon made Leopard forgetful. Later that week, as he watched Sungura's children leaping about outside on the hill, Leopard said to himself, "Small they are, and savory they are!" He licked his lips. "One would be a small mouthful. Three or four would do for a snack. With the parents thrown in for good measure, I wouldn't have to go hunting for days."

The next morning, Sungura's children whimpered and wailed with piercing cries that woke Leopard. He opened his gleaming eyes and snapped his hungry teeth in anticipation.

But through the wall came the clear voice of Sungura shouting, "Wife, what is the matter with these children? Why are they making this racket?"

Sungura's wife replied, clear and high, "Oh, Sungura, your children are starving. They crave leopard meat, and nothing else but a juicy leopard will quiet them."

"What a family!" cried Sungura loudly. "I suppose I shall just have to get them some leopard meat; maybe then they'll be content."

Leopard's lips slipped back over his bared teeth. He flattened himself against the wall and quietly, ever so quietly, began to back out of the house so that Sungura the Mighty Elephant Hunter wouldn't start looking for the nearest leopard to feed his hungry children. He slunk down the side of the hill, belly flat to the ground, as swiftly as he could.

The hares peered out from inside the hut as their fierce neighbor ran off into the bush. "We are safe at last," breathed Sungura's wife.

But she spoke too soon, for within the hour Leopard came back up the hill and beside him was Baboon.

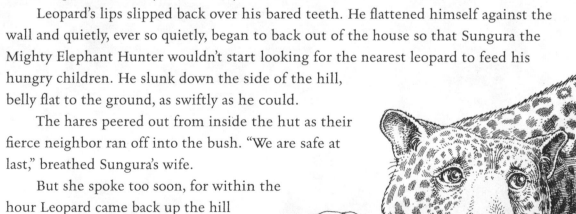

"I tell you, Leopard, hares don't hunt elephants. How could a tiny animal like Sungura do you any harm?"

From the cautious way that Leopard crept up the hill, the Hare family could tell that he still wasn't sure he was safe.

As Baboon and Leopard approached the hut, Sungura said clearly and loudly, "That was very clever of you, Wife, to send Baboon to bring Leopard back. Wipe your tears, children—you will be having leopard for dinner tonight."

Leopard gathered his four paws under him and raced down the hill away from the hut, never to be seen again.

And so it was that Sungura and his family finally had a home of their own.

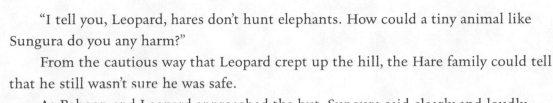

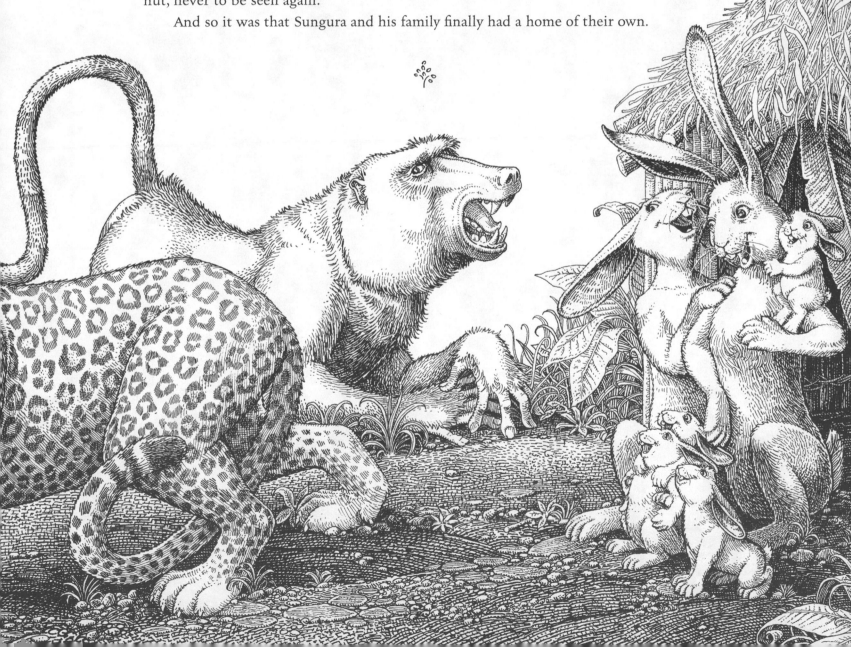

COYOTE and the LITTLE TUNE

Coyote is foremost among the tricksters of Native American storytelling.
This tale comes from the Zuni people of the Southwest.

One day, Coyote was on one of his long expeditions through the forest when he heard the sound of a locust singing from the branch of a piñon tree:

> "Kokopelli has a back with a hump,
> Kokopelli's feet are on back-to-front,
> Kokopelli's playing is very fine—
> And so is mine!"

Over and over, Locust sang this silly little song about the music god. Then he played a few notes on his flute and started over again.

Coyote sat under the piñon tree and listened. Eventually he called up to Locust, "That's a fine song, old friend! Will you teach it to me?"

"Surely," said Locust, pleased that Coyote liked his song.

So he taught it to Coyote and the two of them sang it together—Locust with his high, piping voice and Coyote with his low, growling voice.

"That was wonderful," said Coyote when they had sung the song a few times. "Didn't we sound good together?"

"Oh, yes," said Locust. But secretly he thought that Coyote had the worst voice he had ever heard and that they had sounded terrible together.

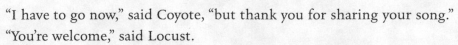

"I have to go now," said Coyote, "but thank you for sharing your song."

"You're welcome," said Locust.

Off went Coyote, humming the song under his breath. He was concentrating so hard on remembering the tune that he didn't see a dead branch in the path. He fell over it, smacking his chin on the dusty ground, and the tune fell out of his head.

I loved that song so much, said Coyote to himself. *I'll just have to go back and ask Locust to teach it to me again.*

So back he went, and there was Locust still sitting in the piñon tree, piping away and singing his little song.

"I'm sorry," said Coyote, "but I fell over a dead branch and hurt myself. Your song went right out of my head. Can you teach it to me again?"

"Of course," said Locust patiently, "but pay attention this time."

Locust sang the song again. "Have you got it now?" he asked.

"Oh, yes," said Coyote. "Thank you so much."

Then he set off again, singing the song over and over to himself so that he wouldn't forget it. He was concentrating so hard on the tune that he didn't see a river in front of him until he fell into it and almost drowned. The shock of the cold water chased the song completely out of his head.

Back he went to Locust.

"I'm really sorry about this, but I fell into a river and forgot your song for the second time! Please sing it to me, just once more."

Locust sighed and sang his song again. "There!" he said. "Try to remember it this time."

"Thank you, I will," said Coyote, and away he went.

This time Coyote got much farther away before a rock fell on his head. It knocked him out cold, and when he came to, he had forgotten the song completely.

"Oh, no!" said Coyote. "Now I shall have to go and ask Locust again. Still, he surely won't mind—he's such a friendly fellow."

So off he went, back to the piñon tree.

Locust, meanwhile, thinking that Coyote would never remember the song and that he was bound to come back and ask for it over and over, decided it was time to play a trick on Coyote the trickster.

Locust was about ready to shed his shell, which had become too tight for him. So he took it off and put a shiny pebble inside it and laid it on the branch of the piñon tree. It looked just like a real locust.

"That ought to fool Coyote," said Locust, and he flew off into another tree to watch and wait. Soon enough, there was the old trickster, loping back.

"Old friend," he called out when he got to the tree. "I'm sorry to trouble you again, but I had an accident. A rock fell on my head and knocked your song out of it. Was it about Corn Maiden? Or Dragonfly? Or was it about Winged Serpent? I just can't remember."

Well, of course he got no answer from the shell. Locust sat on his branch and laughed quietly to himself.

"Hey," shouted Coyote. "Come on. Sing your song for me one last time."

Still he got no answer.

"I'm starting to get angry!" yelled Coyote. "Sing that song for me, or I'll come up there and eat you!"

Still the locust shell was silent.

"Right, then," said Coyote. He jumped up into the piñon tree and seized the shell in his jaws and crunched as hard as he could. Then he began to howl in pain, because the stone inside the shell had broken one of his sharp front teeth.

Coyote couldn't understand what had happened. He ran off, still howling, and didn't come back that way for a long time.

"Never try to teach a song to an idiot," muttered Locust, and he went back to playing his flute and singing his little song:

> "Kokopelli has a back with a hump,
> Kokopelli's feet are on back-to-front,
> Kokopelli's playing is very fine—
> And so is mine!"

CHAUNTECLEER'S DREAM

*The story of Chauntecleer and Pertelote was famously told
by the English writer Geoffrey Chaucer in the* Canterbury Tales,
but this European trickster tale is far older than that.

In the small yard of a poor widow lived the noble rooster Chauntecleer. Well respected throughout the neighborhood, and king of the chicken run, Chauntecleer had a magnificent voice. His morning call was so regular that people trusted the rooster's crow more than the chiming of the church bell.

Chauntecleer had seven wives, but his favorite was Pertelote, the smooth-feathered red hen who adored her golden husband with his coral-red comb and fine black legs.

Now it happened one day, just before dawn, that Pertelote opened one eye to see Chauntecleer beside her on the perch shaking and groaning deep in his throat.

"Whatever is the matter, dearest? Why aren't you outside, crowing your dawn call?"

"Darling wife, I have just had the most terrible dream. I was walking up and down our yard when a beast grabbed me and would have murdered me. It was like a hound, not quite red and not quite yellow, its ears and tail tipped with black. Between horrible glowing eyes was a small snout and a mouth full of sharp teeth, open wide to swallow me up!" Chauntecleer shuddered, his feathers drooping. "It must have been a sign—I'm doomed!"

Pertelote hated seeing her husband in such a state, so she tried to cheer him up. "Depend upon it, husband dearest—this dream is nothing but an evil mood—your heart is usually so merry! Let me make you some tea from the herbs that grow in the hedge.

Then you shall have some worms and dogwood berries. That will warm your heart and get rid of your sadness. You shouldn't be afraid of a silly dream!"

Chauntecleer shook his head. "But wife, there are many stories about people who dream of danger and then ignore the warning, like the man who dreamed of drowning, but ignored his dream and sailed on a ship bound for foreign parts. As soon as the ship left the harbor, its timbers broke and down he went. Surely I should pay attention to this dream!"

Seeing how glum her brave husband was, Pertelote began to pout. "I never thought I would be married to a coward!" she said. "How can I respect you? How can I love you, when you are scared of a tiny little dream?"

At this, Chauntecleer smoothed his feathers and proudly straightened his drooping comb. "Wife, you are right," he said. "Let's be merry while the sun shines! I will take your advice and ignore this dream." And out he strode, making his golden song ring across the yard. Then he pecked up some grains of wheat, and as he chewed them, he became a happier rooster.

One morning, about a month later, Russell the Fox found a gap in the hedge and crept through. Lying hidden in a bed of herbs near the yard, he waited for a chance to ambush the golden rooster.

Chauntecleer was in the yard as usual, singing his morning song. He had forgotten his dream, at least in the daytime; it was only at night that he turned and groaned, remembering the horror of that nightmare. But now, watching his hens, Chauntecleer glowed with happiness. Then he saw the fox, lying flat in the herb bed, and would have fled, but fear made him hesitate.

Knowing he had been seen, Russell the Fox spoke up: "Good sir, don't run away—
I am your friend. I've come a very long way just to hear you sing. I am told that your
voice has more melody than an angel's . . . but then that comes from your noble family.
You know, your father and mother both have been in my house—I knew them well—
both beautiful singers! The way your father used to stretch out his neck and croon, it
brought a tear to my eye. I've come to see if you're as good as he was."

Charmed by this flattery, Chauntecleer forgot to run away. He drew himself up,
puffed out his chest, and stretched his neck to show off his magnificent voice. But no
sooner had he begun his song than the fox sprang forward and grabbed him by the throat,
then pulled the terrified rooster through the gap in the hedge, back toward his den.

It was Pertelote who raised the alarm. Her dearest love, her kingly husband, was taken, so she screamed a queenly squawk that would have raised the dead.

"Chauntecleer, my lovely lord! Oh, Chauntecleer is taken!"

The other hens joined her, their cries ringing out across the yard: "Our lord is taken! Our lord is taken! After that fox!"

Soon the whole neighborhood was in an uproar. The dogs were barking. The poor widow tore out of the house, still holding her spindle and yarn. The cow and her calf bounded along after her—even the pigs from the sty leaped up, terrified by the dog's barking. The ducks waddled after their mistress, and the geese flew out of the tree, hissing angrily. The din was so great, a swarm of bees left their hive and joined the chase.

Russell the Fox ran up the hillside toward the wood with a heaving heart and the rooster lodged firmly between his teeth. Chauntecleer was still alive, but knew that he did not have long. Thinking quickly, he used his magnificent voice: "If I were you, Sir Fox, I would stop and eat me here by this wood, or you may lose your dinner."

The fox spat the rooster out and replied, "I think you are right, Sir Rooster. I'll follow your advice!"

But no sooner had Russell's grip loosened than Chauntecleer flew up into a tree, safely out of the fox's reach.

Outfoxed, Russell began again in his most flattering tones: "Oh, Chauntecleer, I've done you harm, scaring you by taking you from your yard. But I by no means did it to hurt you. Come down again, and you will see that it was only your singing, not your tasty body, that I was interested in!"

"Curse us both if I let you fool me yet again!" said Chauntecleer, glad to keep his golden feathers. "Your flattery will never make me so proud and careless again."

Just then, the widow came over the hillside, followed by the cow and the calf, the dogs and the ducks, the geese and the bees. Their angry shouts were so loud that Russell the Fox ran away into the darkness of the wood, never to be seen again.

So it happened that Chauntecleer escaped from the jaws of the fox and was carried home in triumph to his loving wife. And from that day on, Pertelote was more careful to listen to the dreams of her golden husband.

FROG and CROW

*This story is told in Tibet and shows that even the humble frog
can be smarter than its oldest enemy.*

Once, Crow caught a fat frog and flew to the top of a high roof to eat him. As she
landed, Frog laughed loudly.

"I don't think you have anything to laugh about," said Crow. "What makes you
so merry?"

"Ah, excuse me, Madam Crow," said Frog calmly. "I was just thinking to myself that
this roof is where my father, Frog the Fearsome, lives. When he hears I have been hurt,
he will not rest until he has ripped the culprit limb from limb."

Crow grew quite nervous at the thought of a vengeful Frog the Fearsome. She
hopped down into the gutter of the roof so she would be hidden while she prepared
her meal. Just as she was about to begin, Frog gave a hiccuping chuckle.

"What amuses you so much now?" demanded Crow angrily.

"Oh, nothing really," said Frog with an unruffled smile. "Just that my mighty
uncle, Giant Frog, lives in this very gutter. If anyone tried to hurt me here, he would
surely squash the offender flat."

Fearful of the monstrous Giant Frog, Crow flew farther off to a nearby wellhead.
She dropped Frog on the ground and held him there with one strong claw. As she
raised her beak to strike, Frog coughed a polite cough.

"Madam Crow, I believe that your beak needs to be quite sharp to open my thick
skin. Why don't you sharpen it on that stone over there?"

Distractedly, Crow took two or three hops away to sharpen her beak as suggested.
As soon as Crow's back was turned, Frog made one enormous jump and landed on
top of the wellhead itself.

When she returned from sharpening her beak, Crow found Frog paddling serenely in the well water.

"Oh, good!" she said. "I thought I'd lost you. My beak is quite sharp enough to pierce your wretched hide now. Come up and be eaten!"

"Ah, Madam Crow," said Frog, pleasantly paddling about. "I'm so sorry I can't come and see you, but I don't seem to be able to get out of this well. Why don't you come down and get me?"

But each time Crow flew down the well, Frog dived deeper into the water—so she never did get her dinner!

TRICKS and TRUTHS

Acheria the Fox is one of the best-known tricksters of the Basque people.

Acheria the Fox was so hungry that his growling belly was driving him crazy. When he saw a shepherd herding his sheep along the road, he decided to follow him. He watched the man put the sheep in a pen, then go into his house and start making delicious cheese.

Acheria began to drool when he smelled the cheese. He had to have some. So the trickster found his old friend Wolf and they hatched a plan. That night, Wolf would hide in the trees outside the shepherd's house and howl and howl until the shepherd rushed out to save his flock. Then Acheria would run inside and steal the cheese.

All went as planned. Wolf hid and howled, the shepherd ran out into the night, and Acheria slipped into his house and stole a big bowl full of fresh cheese.

When he was a safe distance away from the house, Acheria began to think. He was far too hungry to share the cheese with Wolf. Very carefully, he took the skin off the top and ate all the juicy cheese underneath. Then he filled up the bowl with earth, put the skin back, and waited for Wolf to come and join him.

When Wolf arrived, Acheria brought out the bowl and put it down between them.

"Let's divide the cheese equally between us," he said. "One of us should have the top—which I think is the best bit—and the other can have the bottom."

"Well," said Wolf, who knew how cunning Acheria was, "I prefer the bottom. You can have the top."

So Acheria lapped all the skin off the top, leaving only the earth for Wolf.

Hungry Wolf was far from pleased, as you can guess, but all Acheria said was, "I am so sorry, my friend! But it's not my fault if the shepherd makes his cheese like this." And away he went, his tummy well filled.

The next day, Acheria saw a boy pass by with food for his father's dinner. Acheria's eyes gleamed with a clever idea, so off he went in search of his old partner, Blackbird.

"Hey, friend," he said, "I know a way we can both get a good dinner tonight."

"How's that?" asked Blackbird.

"If you sit in the road when that boy passes with food for his father and pretend to be hurt, he will try to catch you. Keep hopping along ahead of him, and pretty soon he'll put down his basket so that he can catch you. Then I will steal the food and we can meet up later and share it."

Blackbird thought this was an excellent idea and did as Acheria suggested. Everything went according to plan, and when the boy put down his basket of food to chase the bird, Acheria jumped out and carried it off to his den, where he soon ate every last crumb.

Acheria lay there, full of food, thinking, "Now I have two enemies—Wolf and Blackbird. I'd better leave this part of the forest and cross the river."

So off he went to the riverbank and began to look for a way across. Soon he saw

a boatman passing and called out to him, "Hey! If you take me across the river, I'll tell you three important truths."

"Very well," said the boatman.

Acheria jumped into the boat and said, "People say bread made with rye is better than bread made with wheat, but that's not true. Wheat bread is far better. That's the first truth."

When they reached the middle of the river, Acheria said: "People often say what a fine night it is—as clear as day. That's a lie. Day is always clearer than night. And that's the second truth."

At last the boat reached the far side of the river.

"Now for the third truth," said Acheria. "You're wearing a really bad pair of trousers— and you won't get any better ones until you get passengers who pay you better than I do!"

Then he ran away as quickly as possible. You see—I was that boatman, and I have never forgotten Acheria's three truths.

RAVEN and CRAYFISH

This tale is from the great northern lakes of Siberia.

Flying home to his nest one day, Raven spied a succulent crayfish swimming in the lake below. He swooped down and caught the fat crayfish in his beak, thinking of the feast he would have when he came to his treetop home.

Crayfish was terrified. Knowing that she was seconds away from becoming a raven's dinner, she began to speak as calmly and sweetly as she could: "Oh, great and powerful Raven! I'm so pleased to meet you. You know, I had supper with your father and mother a little while ago. What a delightful couple!"

"Ugoo," said Raven, because his beak was firmly shut, holding tight to his dinner.

"And I have often noticed how enchanting your brothers and sisters are. What a handsome family!" continued Crayfish.

"Ymm-ugoo," said Raven, his beak clamped shut, looking forward to suppertime.

"Of course, they are all majestic," said Crayfish, "but none is your equal. You are the cleverest raven. . . . No, that is not enough. You are the cleverest creature of all creatures since the world's creation."

Delighted by this flattery, Raven opened his beak to agree. Before he could say a word, Crayfish wriggled free and fell back into the lake below, disappearing into the deep, dark water. That night, the cleverest creature of all creatures since the world's creation had to go without his dinner.

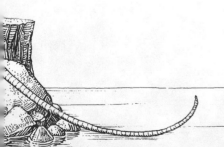

REVENGE IS SWEET

This Cossack tale from Russia features a whole gang of creatures—
but as usual, it is Fox who comes out on top.

There was once a cat who had grown too old, blind, and toothless to catch mice and so his master, the thrifty peasant, put old Cat into a bag and heartlessly left him in the middle of the forest all alone. Along came Fox, who heard Cat's pathetic meows. With one flick of her claws, she opened the sack and let Cat out.

"What were you doing in there, Master Puss?" asked Fox.

Blinking in the bright light, Cat said, "My master abandoned me because I can't catch mice anymore. He didn't want to kill me himself, but he left me here to die."

"Well, never you mind, Master Puss. Though you've seen better days, I can tell you are a wise animal. We will make a good team, you and I. Come with me and I'll help you, if you'll help me."

"Mistress Fox, it will be my delight," said Cat, and away they went.

Fox was as good as her word and built Cat a little house of his own. Then she went to the other animals of the forest to spread some gossip. Although the animals liked to hear her news, they were wary of Fox, who had stolen from them and tricked them many times. Fox told Hare, Bear, Wolf, Boar, and Rabbit all about the peasant's ungrateful treatment of Cat. Though they had never seen a cat before, they were filled with indignation when they heard the story. But they still didn't trust Fox, so after she had gone, they started planning.

Bear was the clever one. "Now, we cannot let this peasant get away with what he has done," he said. "But I don't trust that fox one inch. Let's teach them both a lesson. I'll go and steal the honey mead from the peasant's barrel. Hare, you can steal his ham.

Wolf, you will steal the dripping bowl. Boar can root up his fruit trees, and Rabbit, you can invite Fox and Cat to dinner. Then we can honor Cat and get even with the peasant. And as for Fox, we'll make a pie full of sharpened bones for her. She's so greedy, she'll swallow it in one gulp—you'll see!"

While the other animals were teaching the peasant a lesson, Rabbit went very humbly to Fox and Cat and begged the honor of their company at dinner.

The table was set, piled high with all the good things stolen from the peasant's house: plump ham, rich drippings, juicy apples and pears, and the sweet delight of honey mead.

The forest animals welcomed Cat as their guest of honor, giving Fox a more humble place at the bottom of the table. Fox sat meekly next to the bone pie, waiting to be served. Bear sat Cat next to the ham and offered him a slice.

"Meow, meow," said Cat in a muffled tone, chewing.

"What did he say?" asked the Bear behind his paw to the other animals. "It sounded like 'Too small, too small.' What an ungrateful animal to sneer at our hard-stolen food! He must be a monster to have such a great appetite."

The forest animals began to be afraid of Cat, who ate and ate as if he had never eaten before. In each of their minds was the same thought: Was this why the peasant had abandoned him in the wood? Meanwhile, Fox sat politely, waiting to be invited to eat.

The food cheered up Cat, and he peered blindly around the table. Seeing Boar's bristly snout, Cat thought it was a mouse. The fur went up on his back and tail until Cat was twice his ordinary size. He gathered himself to spring and, although he was

old and feeble, there was nothing wrong with his voice, so he began to spit and yowl: "Spspts yar-rrowl! Krtrsts-yooowl!"

"Quick, run and hide!" cried Bear. "He really is a monster!"

Bear, Rabbit, Wolf, Boar, and Hare jumped up and ran away as fast as they could.

Fox sprang onto the table and slurped up the honey mead, while Cat gobbled up the drippings. Never had two animals been so sticky and full of food.

As they rolled home together, licking their paws, so full that they could hardly stand, Fox said to Cat, "Thanks for your help, Master Puss. I knew that you would be helpful to me. Now we are safe and well fed, while those sneaking animals have not only punished your old master but have also learned respect for Fox and Cat. What a great team we are!"

And when the forest animals crept back to the clearing, there was nothing left on that table but an uneaten pie full of bones.

LION and UNICORN

*This story was first written down in the fourteenth century
by John of Sheppey, from Kent, England.*

Lion and Unicorn had been enemies for so long that neither of them could remember how or when they had first started to argue. Whenever they met, one always tried to outwit the other. But as the years went by, they both grew old and feeble in limb.

One day, Lion pretended to be older and sicker than he was. He limped over to where Unicorn lived. In a whining, shaky voice, he said, "My old enemy, let us make a truce and end the fighting between us. As you can see, I can't harm anyone anymore."

Unicorn looked at his old enemy, surprised to see tears in Lion's eyes. "What do you want with me?" he asked suspiciously.

"I have come to you," said Lion, "because I am near the end of my days. Before I die, I want to say good-bye to my old wife, who lives far out in the desert. I don't think I can get there in time unless I have a walking stick to lean on. So you see, I've come to ask you to lend me your horn. It's thick and sturdy and exactly the right length for me to walk with. I promise I'll return it to you as soon as I've seen my wife and said good-bye to her."

Putting on his most pathetic expression, Lion let a single tear roll down his cheek. "Perhaps old enemies can become old friends?" he said, lifting a feeble paw to wipe away the tear.

Unicorn was touched by this speech and at once removed his horn and gave it to Lion. But he had forgotten that without a horn, a unicorn is nothing more than a white horse, with only his speed and sharp hooves to defend himself.

As soon as Lion held the horn in his mighty paws, he sprang onto Unicorn and plunged it deeply into his old enemy's side.

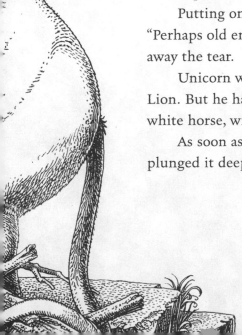

Unicorn lay panting on the ground and cried, "You are not only cruel but a lying cheat as well! How could you repay my goodwill with such wickedness?"

Lion only laughed. "Fool! Don't you know the old saying—whoever preserves the life of his enemy steals his own strength? You should know that mercy is pointless between old enemies like us."

Unicorn, who also knew many wise sayings, answered, "It is also said that victory is won by honor."

Then he sent his beautiful voice to each of the four directions. "Let all creatures know that I fell victim to a treacherous truce," he proclaimed. "I die with honor."

But Lion had the last word. As he took the life of his old enemy, he roared, "Those who don't protect themselves from their enemies, even when they seem weak and humble, have no protection at all!"

The Making
of the World

*Winabijou is the great trickster of the Ojibwa people
of North America.*

In the time before our world began, Winabijou the Hare lived with his adopted brother, Wolf. One day Wolf went out hunting and fell through a hole in the ice into the Lands Below, where the Serpent Gods lived in the dark and cold. The Serpent Gods were so angry at Wolf for trespassing into their world that they caught him and killed him.

Now, the days passed and Wolf didn't return, so Winabijou set off to track Wolf's footprints over the snowy ground. He found the prints of geese, moose, and beavers, but all of these tracks led back to their homes—all except Wolf's, which led to the hole in the ice.

"Oh, my brother!" Winabijou wept, realizing what had happened. Then he grew angry and decided that he wanted revenge for the death of his adopted brother. So he called upon the Thunder Gods of the Lands Above to send the warmth of summer early, to make the Serpent Gods come out of the Lands Below. The sun grew stronger and began to melt the snow covering the land.

Winabijou searched for Wolf's body in the melting snows so that he could bury him honorably. He saw Kingfisher chewing something and asked what she was eating.

"Oh," the bird said, "just a bit of a wolf that the Serpent Gods killed in their cave below."

Winabijou was angry, but he kept his temper and asked quietly, "Tell me, do the Serpent Gods ever come out of their cave?"

"Oh, yes," Kingfisher said. "They usually bask on the sunny rocks over there. But they are protected by their guards—snakes, lizards, and turtles."

Winabijou gave Kingfisher a necklace of shells for his help, which is why kingfishers still have a white band around their throats. But angry Winabijou could not keep his temper at the sight of the bird chewing on his brother, Wolf, so he grabbed at Kingfisher. Fast as a flash, Kingfisher flew away, so Winabijou caught only a tuft of feathers—which is why kingfishers have only a raised crest of feathers on their heads instead of a full plume.

With Kingfisher's information, Winabijou planned how he would play a great trick on the Serpent Gods. He prayed all night to the Thunder Gods of the Land Above, asking them to make the next days sunny, and armed himself with a bow and arrows. Then he hid by the rocks, turning himself into an old tree stump.

Finally it was time for the Serpent Gods to come out. First came their bodyguards—snakes, lizards, and turtles, who moved in every direction. Then the Serpent Gods began to appear, taking the form of bears, to enjoy the sunny day. One became a great white bear, the other a huge brown one.

"I never saw that stump before," said Brown Bear.

"You probably did not notice it; I'm sure it has always been there," said White Bear.

"I'm not sure," said Brown Bear thoughtfully, and with his savage claws he scratched deep grooves in the stump that was Winabijou.

Like a brave warrior, poor Winabijou stifled his cries as Brown Bear sharpened his claws upon him. He held his bow and arrows tightly so that no one would suspect that he wasn't really a tree stump.

"Let me see," said Boa Constrictor, one of the snake guards. He wound himself around the stump that was Winabijou three or four times, squeezing hard. Poor Winabijou was nearly choked to death, but by puffing out his chest, he kept a little breath in his body.

"It really is just a stump," said White Bear.

"Let's take a nap, then," agreed Brown Bear, lying down on the sunny rocks.

When they were both asleep, Winabijou shot Brown Bear in the chest and White Bear in the stomach.

"You're the ones who killed my brother!" he shouted. So fierce was his cry that the wounded bears and their guards jumped into the river and dug down into their cave in the Lands Below.

Winabijou knew he had done a terrible thing—he had attacked the gods from the Lands Below. He took some reeds and made a hat to disguise his long ears, then set off down the road. A little way along, he met with old Toad Healer, who was carrying a bundle of bark. She recognized him at once. "You're Winabijou!" she cried.

"No, I'm not!" the hare told her. "If I were really Winabijou, what do you think would be happening right now?"

Old Toad Healer looked doubtful. "Well, since Winabijou shot the gods from the Lands Below, they'd be punishing him terribly. So I suppose you can't be him."

"Where are you off to, anyway?" asked Winabijou.

"I'm off to the Lands Below, to draw out the arrows Winabijou shot into the gods."

"And what are you going to do with all that bark?" the hare asked.

"I'm going to make string; then with the help of the Gods Below, we will wind it all around the world. If Winabijou should touch even one strand of it, the Gods Below will know it and they will send a great flood to drown him."

Winabijou smiled a sad and terrible smile and hit her on the head with a big tree root. Then he took her leathery hide and dressed himself in it. In his new disguise, he set off to the home of the Serpent Gods. Because the summer had come early, they now lived in a lodge above the ground.

Thinking that it was old Toad Healer coming to heal their masters, the turtle sentries did not challenge Winabijou. The hare saw with almost uncontrollable rage and sorrow that they had hung the hide of his brother, Wolf, over the door. But he pushed down his anger and meekly trotted forward.

Making his voice sound like the old healer, Winabijou sang, "I've come to draw the arrows. Everyone, get out of this lodge now—I have a new way to heal and I need as much space as possible."

All the guards left the lodge, and Winabijou took hold of the arrows that stuck out of the Serpent Gods, who were lying on the table. Winabijou turned and pushed those arrows in deeper and deeper, until the gods were nearly dead.

Then he ran from the lodge, grabbing hold of the hide of his brother Wolf from over the door as he went. As he raced away, the guards ran after him and the Serpent Gods, with their last breath, called upon the waters to rise. Winabijou shot one look backward, saw the flood coming, and ran to higher ground. But still the waters followed.

He came to Badger's den and shouted, "I promise that I will award you stripes of honor if you will let me into your den!"

Badger grudgingly agreed, but even in the most secret tunnels of his underground home, the waters began to trickle in. Winabijou had to flee, leaving Badger forever afterward with the stripes of honor upon his face.

Winabijou reached the highest peak of the tallest hill, where a single pine tree stood. "Please," he panted, "let me into your branches."

"Because of your crimes we will all be killed," said the pine tree, but it let Winabijou climb up.

Soon the floodwaters were almost above Winabijou's gasping mouth, and he begged the tree, "Please, please, stretch just a little more." The pine tree rose up to four times its own height, but finally it said, "That is as far as I can go, Winabijou."

Now this was the worst fix Winabijou had ever been in. The waters had reached up to his mouth and then stopped, but he had to heave himself up to get every breath.

The top of the pine tree said, "Ah, Winabijou, the trick is on you now! This is your punishment for killing the Serpent Gods!"

Winabijou could do nothing. The flood was at its height, and all the water animals were swimming or floating on the surface because there was no dry land to rest upon.

Then the hare shook himself. He called to a loon nearby, "Sister Loon, please swim down to the depths and bring me up some earth."

But Loon dived down too deep, and when she came floating back up to the surface of the flood, there was no life in her. Winabijou blew some of his precious breath into her body and she came back to life.

"Hey, Brother Otter! Swim to the depths and bring me a little earth!" said the hare.

The otter dived down, but the earth was too far under the water and he too floated lifelessly back to the surface. Again, Winabijou blew some of his precious breath into the body of Otter and he came back to life.

"Brother Muskrat! Go and dive to the depths and bring me a little earth!"

The muskrat dived deeper than any of the other animals and was nearly out of breath when his paws were able to scrabble just a little earth. He swam up to the surface of the flood, nearly choking. Winabijou breathed gently upon him and took the earth from Muskrat's claws. He squeezed it together into a ball and held it up in the sunshine to dry until his whole body ached. Then he threw it out over the water.

Some of the animals who were still alive called to Winabijou, "What use is it to make anything? We are all going to drown. Leave your tricks, Winabijou, and get ready to die with dignity."

"The trick is not over yet," said Winabijou with a weak smile. He pointed to where he had thrown the little ball of earth. Where it had landed, the earth had become an island.

With great relief, all the water animals swam for the island. Winabijou rewarded the diving animals by giving them food: Muskrat had rushes; Loon was given mud from the shore; Otter was given fish. Other animals had survived the flood by floating on branches and logs. Winabijou sent Fox to measure the island.

On the first day, Fox came back quickly because the island was still small. On the second day, Fox took longer to run around it because the island was growing. On the tenth day, Fox never returned because the island had grown to its present size. That is why you can still see foxes trotting around the shoreline.

Then Winabijou prayed and sang to the Gods Above and the Gods Below to come and inhabit the new land that he had made, for it was ready for all things to live on. And it seems they must have forgiven him, because this world was his greatest trick— and don't you forget it!

The KING of ALL BIRDS

This contest of the birds comes from a traditional story told in Ireland.

Long ago, in the ages before men, the birds assembled to elect one of their number to be King of All Birds.

There was a great cawing and crying and flashing of wings as every species of bird jostled to represent their own kind at this parliament. Gull was there, as were Kingfisher, Crow, Swallow, Swan—and so many more that to tell you all of them would take days.

"How shall we decide who is most worthy?" asked Crane, standing on one tall leg.

Wise Owl replied, "Every bird has wings to fly freely about the sky. Since the air is our element, let our king be the one who flies the highest."

So it was agreed. The contest would be easy to judge, since one bird would clearly beat all others in the sight of witnesses. Into the clear sky of morning, one member of each bird clan rose up on proud wings.

The first to tire were the plump birds like Pheasant and Chicken. Then, as the small songbirds like Robin and Finch rose higher, they grew slower and slower until they were forced to fall back.

Even the strong-winged Swallow and Goose, who can fly far over land and sea, were defeated by the height.

Almost at the very limits of the sky, high-flying Lark ceased her song and fell back down to earth. Then the smaller Hawks bucked in the fierce winds and descended with drooping tails.

Finally, only Eagle was left, soaring above all the others into the highest heights on his strong wings.

"I shall be your king!" he boomed, seeing no others above him.

"Not so," said a little voice. "I am above you."

"Who speaks?" cried Eagle, turning back his stern head in amazement.

"It is me!" said little Wren, flying just above Eagle's head. Wren had been curled up safely between the eagle's huge wings until the great bird had exhausted himself.

The proud eagle was forced to admit, since the little bird was indeed higher than he, that Wren really was the King of All Birds.

This is why one of the smallest birds of the hedge is honored still, and why, to this very day, at the turning of midwinter, we sing a song that goes:

"The wren, the wren, the King of All Birds!"

PARTNERS

In Finnish folklore, Mikka the Fox and Pekka the Wolf are old friends,
but somehow Pekka almost always comes off worse.

Pekka the Wolf and Mikka the Fox were old friends who lived close to each other on the edge of an old, dark forest. One day they decided to enter into a partnership.

"The first thing we should do," said Pekka the Wolf, "is make a clearing in the forest so that we can plant crops."

"An excellent idea!" said Mikka the Fox, and off they went to work, each of them taking a big pot of butter for his lunch. They left the butter in a nearby stream to keep cool and then started working.

Mikka soon tired of the hard business of felling trees. He made an excuse to leave for a while, and when he came back, he said to Pekka, "I just heard that the farmer and his wife are having a christening today. Of course they asked me to come."

"What a shame," said Pekka the Wolf. "If we didn't have all this work to do, you could go."

"I really should," said Mikka, sighing mightily. "The farmer and his family are such good neighbors that we don't want to insult them."

"Very well," said Pekka, "but don't stay long—we have a lot to do."

So off went Mikka the Fox, but only as far as the stream where the two animals had left their butter. He took out Pekka's pot and licked off the top. Then he ran back to where Pekka the Wolf was still hard at work cutting down trees.

"Hello, Mikka," said his friend. "How was the christening?"

"Wonderful! Wonderful!" said Mikka the Fox.

"What did they name the child?" asked Pekka.

"They called her Top," said Mikka quickly.

"That's a strange name," said Pekka.

"Well, anyway, I just came to see how you are doing," said Mikka the Fox quickly. "Now I have to go back to the farm."

"What for?" demanded Pekka the Wolf. "We still have so much work to do."

"Didn't I tell you?" asked Mikka innocently. "There is a second christening. The farmer's daughter has had a baby too. I have to go, or they will be so upset."

"Don't be long," said Pekka the Wolf with a sigh.

So off went Mikka the Fox again, but again he didn't go far. He stopped at the stream, where he got the wolf's pot of butter and licked out the middle. Then he hurried back.

"There you are," said Pekka. "How was the christening this time?"

"Lovely! Lovely!" said Mikka the Fox.

"And what did they name the child this time?"

"Oh, they called him Middle," said Mikka quickly.

"Another strange name," said Pekka.

Now Mikka made a great fuss of helping, but before long he grew tired again and said, "I'm really sorry, old friend, but I must go back to the farm one more time."

"What for *now*?" demanded Pekka the Wolf. "Surely there can't be another christening!"

"Oh, but there is," said Mikka the Fox. "The farmer's other daughter has had a baby and they were most insistent that I should be there. I promise I won't be long."

And off he went, straight back to the stream. He ate the rest of Pekka's butter, then hurried back to where the wolf had almost finished cutting down the trees.

"There you are at last," grumbled Pekka. "How was the christening this time?"

"Wonderful! Wonderful!" answered Mikka.

"And what name did they give the child?"

"They called her Bottom," said Mikka.

"They certainly do choose strange names," said Pekka.

Mikka pretended to work hard for a few minutes after that. Then he threw himself down with a yawn.

"It must be time for dinner," he said. Pekka the Wolf agreed, starving from all his hard work, and the two friends hurried back to the stream and took out their pots of delicious cool butter.

"What's this?" cried Pekka. "Mine is all gone! Did you eat it?" He looked suspiciously at Mikka the Fox.

"Me?" answered Mikka. "How could I? You know I've been up at the farm all day and when I wasn't there I was working next to you. You must have eaten it yourself."

"Of course I haven't eaten it!" shouted the wolf. "I'm sure it must have been you."

"Pekka, I won't have you thinking such a thing!" cried Mikka angrily. "We must get to the bottom of this. Here's what I suggest: Let's both lie down in the sun for a while. The heat will make the butter melt. If I ate it, it will run out of my nose. If it runs out of your own nose, we will know it was you."

Pekka the Wolf agreed, and the two animals lay down. Pekka was so tired from his labors that he fell asleep almost at once. Mikka the Fox got up quietly and dabbed a spot of butter on the wolf's nose. Then as the hot sun melted it, he shook his old friend awake.

"Look, Pekka, there's butter running out of your nose. It must have been you who ate it."

"I certainly don't remember eating it," said Pekka miserably. "I must be working too hard."

"Well, now you know it wasn't me," said crafty Mikka, looking hurt. "You really shouldn't be so quick to suspect me."

The two animals went back to the clearing. Pekka the Wolf began to collect all the wood he had felled so they could burn it.

Mikka went off and lay down behind some bushes.

"Hey, Mikka, aren't you going to help me?" called Pekka.

"I'm just keeping watch to make sure no sparks fly over here," said Mikka. "We don't want to burn down the whole forest."

So poor, hard-working Pekka the Wolf burned up all the wood and soon there was a thick layer of ash for them to plant seeds in.

"Come on, Mikka, aren't you going to help me with the planting?" grumbled Pekka.

"You'd better do it," answered Mikka from his resting place behind the bushes. "I'll keep watch for birds and make sure they don't steal any of our precious seeds."

Then he closed his eyes and began to snooze, while poor, tired Pekka the Wolf, who had cut down all the trees, piled up all the logs, burned them all up, and spread out all the ash, planted the seeds as well.

The time came when the seeds that Pekka the Wolf had planted began to sprout, and soon after that, it was time for harvesting. The two friends cut the grain, carried the sheaves into the threshing barn, and left them out to dry.

When it was time to thresh the grain, they decided to ask Osmo the Bear for help.

"I'd be glad to help you, for a share of the grain," said Osmo.

"Agreed," said Mikka and Pekka. Then, remembering what had happened before, Pekka said, "First we need to agree how we should divide the work."

"That's easy," said Mikka the Fox, climbing up into the rafters of the barn. "I'll stay up here and make sure the roof doesn't fall on you. Don't worry, you can work in safety as long as I'm keeping watch."

So Osmo the Bear and Pekka the Wolf began to work, Osmo whirling the thresher and Pekka separating the chaff from the grain. Every now and then Mikka threw a few small pieces of wood down, and when the two animals called out in alarm, he told them everything was under control, but it was incredibly hard work holding up the roof—he was bound to let a few bits fall.

Osmo and Pekka continued to work until every bit of grain was threshed. Then Mikka the Fox hurried down from the rafters and flung himself on the ground as though exhausted.

"I'm so glad that's over," he said. "I don't think I could have held up that heavy roof much longer!"

"How shall we divide up our harvest?" asked Pekka the Wolf.

"Easy!" cried Mikka. "There are three of us and three heaps of grain. The biggest

should obviously go to Osmo, who is the biggest of us all. The middle-size heap should go to you, Pekka. I'm the smallest so I'll have the little heap."

"Are you sure about that?" asked Pekka the Wolf doubtfully.

"Oh, yes," said Mikka, smiling behind his paw—because he knew, of course, that Osmo, by taking the biggest heap, was just getting the straw; while Pekka, who got the second-largest heap, was getting the chaff, but Mikka himself was getting all the tasty grain.

The three animals went off to the mill to grind their grain into flour. As the millstone turned on Mikka the Fox's grain, it made a rough rasping sound.

"That's odd," said Osmo the Bear to Pekka the Wolf. "Mikka's grain sounds different from ours."

"Try mixing some sand in with yours," said Mikka the Fox at once. "Then it will sound just like mine."

Osmo and Pekka did as Mikka suggested, and now their grain did indeed sound like his. Soon they each had a sack of flour, and each went home feeling very pleased with himself.

The first thing the three friends wanted to do was to see what kind of porridge their flour would make. Osmo the Bear tried first. His porridge came out black and gritty. Puzzled, the bear wandered over to Mikka's house. There he found the fox stirring a pot full of smooth white porridge.

"Why doesn't mine look like that?" demanded Osmo.

"Did you wash your flour before cooking it?" asked Mikka.

"Wash it? No! Was I supposed to?" asked the bear.

"Of course," said Mikka. "Just take it down to the river and drop it in. When it's clean you can make fine porridge."

So Osmo the Bear took his sack of ground-up straw to the river and poured it all in. Of course, it was washed away in minutes and that was the end of Osmo's share.

Pekka the Wolf wasn't doing too well with his porridge either. Soon he made his way to Mikka's house.

"Look how smooth and white your porridge is!" he exclaimed. "I wish mine looked like that. Can I watch you for a while and see how you make it?"

"Of course," said Mikka the Fox. "Why don't you hang your porridge pot next to mine over the fire?"

"Your porridge looks so good and tasty," said Pekka. "What's your secret?"

"Well, before you came, I climbed up and hung over the fire for a while. The heat melted my fat and it dripped down into my porridge, making it smooth and white."

"I'll have to try that," said Pekka the Wolf. He climbed up into the chimney, and stayed there as long as he could. But soon it got too hot and he fell down and singed his fur—which is why wolves smell of burned hair to this day.

But when he tried his porridge, it tasted just as bad.

"I just don't understand it," said Pekka. "Can I taste some of your porridge?"

"Of course," said Mikka the Fox smoothly. But while Pekka was looking the other way he scooped up a big dollop of the wolf's porridge and dropped it on top of his.

"Help yourself," said Mikka. "Take some from there—it's a particularly good bit."

Of course, the bit Mikka pointed to was the dollop of Pekka's own porridge. The miserable wolf swallowed a big spoonful, then spat it out at once.

"Strange. It tastes exactly the same as mine. I just don't think I like porridge anymore."

So off went the poor wolf, leaving Mikka the Fox laughing so hard that he rolled around on the floor.

"I wonder why Pekka doesn't like porridge anymore," he said, helping himself to a huge dollop. "It tastes just fine to me!"

An Ocean Cruise

The stories of Rat, Crab, and Octopus
are told all over the islands of Micronesia.

Rat and Crab lived together on an island in the middle of the ocean. It was so small that they couldn't help meeting each other every day in their search for food. One day Crab stopped and said to Rat, "Look, we are the only two on this island. Let's take turns finding food for both of us every other day, so that we each get a rest."

"Why don't you begin, Crab?" Rat suggested, and he went to find a quiet place to hide from the sun. Crab took her sideways path, and before sunset she snapped her pincers loudly together and called Rat to share in her catch. Rat thrust his long snout into the fish that Crab had found, taking huge mouthfuls and leaving her only a lick of grease.

The next day, it was Rat's turn. He pounced on a family of beetles, ate them quickly, and spat out the wing cases. He dug up a few roots and greedily separated the choice juicy white core from the hard brown casing. Then he dug out the milky flesh of a coconut and left the empty shell full of spent beetle cases and hard brown roots for Crab.

A week passed and Crab was getting sick of Rat's behavior. Every day was the same story—Rat dined well while Crab was left with little or nothing to eat. So, on her rest days, Crab began to carve a canoe with her clever claws. When it was finished, she called out to Rat, "Dear partner, I wonder whether you would like to come on a cruise."

Rat sniffed around the canoe with suspicion. "Won't we need paddles to row this boat?" he asked.

"With my big pincers, I can take care of that," said Crab, who had fashioned a long rudder to steer with.

Rat hated to get wet, but the day was sunny and he had been stuck on the island for a long time, so in he jumped and sat down, keeping his paws tucked up out of the water. Then Crab pushed the canoe into the waves. Rat lay back and let Crab do all the steering through the dangerous reefs into the deep waters of the great blue ocean.

Crab waited until Rat was lazily snoozing in the prow of the canoe, and then with her razor-sharp claws she began to make a hole in the bottom. Water began to gush and bubble into the canoe, and Rat woke from a lovely dream to find that he was alone in the boat and getting steadily wetter.

Through the hole in the canoe's bottom, he saw Crab lowering herself into the ocean. She could breathe underwater, but he could not. She could walk on the ocean bed to dry land, but he couldn't even swim.

Rat set up a wailing cry for help so piteous that a hairy octopus rose from the ocean depths to see what was going on. "What is the trouble, little brother?" asked the huge octopus, who, in addition to his eight arms, had a wonderful crop of hair upon his great head.

"Please take me to the land," begged Rat as the canoe began to sink. "If you do, I will give you a silver mirror."

"What is a mirror?" asked Octopus.

"It is a thing that shows what a wonderfully handsome creature you are," said Rat, now perching on the topmost end of the prow, as it too was being sucked beneath the waves.

"Very well," said the octopus. "Grab onto the back of my head and I will take you to dry land."

Rat sprang onto the back of Octopus's great head, knotting his paws into the thick hair to balance, as Octopus raced through the waves.

The only problem was, what with the long ocean cruise, nearly drowning, and being rescued, Rat was absolutely starving. He tried to open his mouth and catch the flying fish as they sped through the water, but his mouth wasn't big enough. Seeing nothing else to eat, Rat began to nibble at Octopus's long hair.

As moonlight replaced sunlight, they reached the shores of an island, and Octopus shook Rat off onto the rocks. Rat cracked open a fallen coconut, swiftly ate one half of the flesh, and brought the other half to the octopus.

"Here is your mirror!" said Rat, holding the coconut out to Octopus. "Now you can see what a hideously ugly monster you are with your eight arms and your great bald head!"

Clinging to the reef, Octopus peered into the milky mirror and saw a fearful sight reflected in the moonlight: all of his lovely long locks were gone forever! He sank down into the water, ashamed to be seen. And this is why, to this day, the octopus remains bald and hides in the depths of the ocean.

As for Rat, he awoke the next morning to find himself alone on the same island that he had left. And there he is still, waiting for another crab to join him.

A NOSE for a NOSE

This is a story about getting even, from the Uintah Ute people of North America.

Long ago, Wildcat had a long nose and a long, long tail, and Coyote the trickster had a snub nose and a short, short tail. One day, while Wildcat was sleeping upon a warm rock, along came Coyote. After staring hard at his sleeping face, Coyote shoved Wildcat's nose in until it became short. Then he twisted Wildcat's tail in until it became really stubby. "Much better!" he said, and went on his way.

When Wildcat woke up, he was thirsty and went to the creek to drink. Crouching over the water, he saw his own reflection and got a big surprise.

"What's the matter with me?" he shouted, looking sideways at his nose, which had become snubby and short. Then he noticed that his long, graceful tail had gone, replaced by a short, stubby stump sticking out of his rump. He pondered the mystery for a while. "I bet that rascal Coyote has done this!" he muttered.

Wildcat followed Coyote's trail and soon found him, asleep. Wildcat put his claws on either side of Coyote's snout and pulled and pulled until his snout grew long and pointed. Then he went around to Coyote's rump and pulled and pulled until his short, chunky tail was long and thin. "Much better!" said Wildcat, and he strolled off, very satisfied.

When Coyote awoke, he saw that his snout had grown strangely far away and that his tail had become wondrously long and thin. He yawned, scratched, wagged his tail, and smiled.

"Now I can get more into my jaws, howl louder, and wag my tail better than ever!" said Coyote, and he strolled off, very satisfied.

Maybe if Wildcat had pulled a bit harder, this would have been a much longer tale.

VIJAYA and the ELEPHANT'S OATH

Vijaya the Hare and Chaturdanta the Elephant are important characters in Indian storytelling.

Many years ago, in the dry season, when the earth was cracked and dusty, the animals were desperate for water. At the Lake of the Moon, holy place of the Moon God, there was a rush at sunrise as animals big and small jostled at the lake's edge. In the crush, many hares were trodden underfoot by a herd of elephants.

When the Moon God, Silimukha, the Great Hare who lives in the moon, heard this sad news, he was very angry. He called for his ambassador, Vijaya, and said to him, "Go quickly to Chaturdanta, King of the Elephants, and tell him to find another place for his herd to drink. Tell him that there will be a terrible punishment if he does not obey me."

Vijaya, Ambassador of the Hares, was famed for his careful negotiations between animals. He came to the tall shady trees where Chaturdanta sat. Vijaya climbed up on a rock so that the elephant could see him and bowed low.

"Great King of All the Elephants, I am sent to speak to you by my master, Silimukha the Moon God. He is angry that you have defiled the cool waters of his lake and killed the hares who are under his protection."

"If Silimukha can bring the rains, then we will not need to drink at the Lake of the Moon again," said Chaturdanta, listless with the heat. "Doesn't he know that the water holes are nearly empty and the rivers have dried to a mere trickle?"

But Vijaya stood firm. "King Chaturdanta, you must swear that neither you nor your herd will drink there again—or you will be taught a lesson."

"What punishment could be worse than death by thirst?" asked Chaturdanta.

"Silimukha, Lord of Increase and Decrease, can forbid the birth of any new elephants. Without new young, your herds will die out," said Vijaya gravely.

Chaturdanta thought carefully. "Then I swear that no elephant will ever drink at the Lake of the Moon again."

Vijaya knew that Chaturdanta would keep his promise only if he knew that his oath was witnessed.

"Come with me to visit Silimukha, for he has ordered me to bring you into his presence so that he can hear your oath himself."

Vijaya led the great elephant by many roundabout ways, as if they were going to see the Moon God, but the clever hare really took him to the Lake of the Moon.

"Prepare yourself, Chaturdanta," he said in hushed tones. "Few have looked upon the face of the Moon God and lived to tell the tale. Prepare yourself to gaze upon his glorious majesty and make your oath again."

By this time darkness had fallen and the lake was still and quiet.

"Close your eyes, Great Elephant," whispered Vijaya, "for you are the first of your kind to come into the presence of the Moon God."

Then Vijaya began to chant an eerie song to the moon, which made the hairs on Chaturdanta's back rise up. Finally, Vijaya led the King of the Elephants into the presence of the Moon God.

"Bow your head, Chaturdanta, and look upon the Moon God as you make your oath."

As Chaturdanta bowed low over the moonlit waters, he slowly opened his eyes and saw the disc of the moon. And there, standing within it, was the Moon God himself— a mighty, shimmering elephant.

Nearly struck silent at the huge size of the sacred being before him, Chaturdanta bowed even lower, swearing that he and his herd would keep their oath and never drink at the lake again.

Then Vijaya led the contrite elephant away, praising him for his great courage at coming into the presence of the Moon God. In his wisdom and cunning, Vijaya had made Chaturdanta swear an oath by the most sacred thing the elephant understood— his own image reflected in the water.

And ever after, when Silimukha sent the rains to cool the earth, Chaturdanta told his people, "You see, the Great One who lives in the moon really is an elephant!"

The
COLDEST NIGHT

This is an ancient tale from Ireland.

When the world was younger than it is now, an old eagle named Leithin had her nest on the cliffs near the river Shannon. One night there came such a frost as had never been seen or felt in that part of Ireland. When the morning dawned, red and bitter, Leithin heard two of her nestlings arguing.

"Was there ever a night as cold as last night in all the memory of the world?" said one.

"I don't remember one like it," answered another, "but there is someone who might know."

"And who might that be?" asked Leithin.

"Why, Dubhchosach, the black-footed stag who lives near Ben Bulben," answered the nestling. "I have heard that he has been on the face of the earth since the Great Flood. If anyone knows, he must."

Now Leithin was filled with longing to know the answer to this question, for she herself was of great age and could not believe there had ever been a colder night. So she flew off toward Ben Bulben, though the wind was so strong it blew her about the sky like a leaf, and the cold was as great as ever, so she shivered in spite of her thick feathers. She came to the slopes of Ben Bulben, and there she saw the swift-footed stag scratching his flank against a bare old stump of oak that clung to the hillside.

"Tell me," said Leithin, "did you ever in all your long life know of a night as cold as last night?"

"I have never known one so fierce," answered Dubhchosach.

"And what is your age, wise one?" asked Leithin.

"Do you see this stump of an oak here?" said the stag. "I remember when it was no more than a sapling. I was born on that couch of moss at its foot and reared there until I was full-grown. It was my favorite spot then, as it is today, and I used to return there every night, no matter how far I traveled by day. That old oak and I grew together, until it was a mighty tree that gave shade in summer and shelter from the winter winds. I used to rub against it all the time, scratching my antlers there until the tree grew bare. I rubbed and rubbed until it was worn down to this stump you see here. Yet in all that time I have never seen a night as cold as last night."

So Leithin flew home and told her nestlings what Dubhchosach had said. "It must be," she said, "that no one can remember a night as cold as last night." But the nestling who had spoken up before said, "There is one older than Dubhchosach."

"And who is that?" demanded Leithin.

"That would be Dubhgoire, the Blackbird of Clonfert," answered the bird. "He is sure to know the answer."

"Then I shall go and ask this ancient one," said Leithin.

The next morning she set out again, though the weather was as bad as ever and snow gathered on her wings. It was a long journey to Clonfert, but Leithin found her way there and watched as the blackbirds roosted in the bare trees. Soon she saw one that stood out from all the rest, for its wings were white.

As Leithin watched, this bird flew down into a hole beneath the roof of a little hut. Leithin followed it and found herself inside a forge—its fires were dead and the blacksmith long gone.

"Are you Dubhgoire the Blackbird?" asked Leithin.

"I am," replied the blackbird. Close up he looked like the most ancient creature, his feathers tattered and his wings pure white.

"I am Leithin, from the cliffs near the Shannon. I have come to ask you a question."

"Ask away," croaked Dubhgoire.

"Two nights since was the coldest night I can remember, and I have lived many years. Already I have asked the Stag of Ben Bulben and even he cannot remember a worse one. Tell me, can you remember a colder night?"

The blackbird was silent for a moment, then he fluttered down to the ground and perched on an ancient anvil.

"I was born in this forge, and when I was a fledgling, this anvil was whole and unworn. Do you see how it is all worn away on this side? Well, that is with the rubbing of my beak against the iron. In my lifetime I have worn it away to a thin sliver. Yet never in all that time have I seen or felt a colder night than the one which came two nights ago."

Having found her answer, Leithin spread her wings and flew back to her nest.

"What have you to tell us today?" asked the nestling who had started the quest.

"I have flown all the way to Clonfert, and there I spoke with Dubhgoire. Though he has lived there long enough to wear away an iron anvil with his beak, even he cannot remember a worse night than that of two nights ago. It must be true—it really was the coldest night."

"Ha! There is one still older than Dubhgoire," cried the bird. "Goll, the half-blind Salmon of Assaroe, would definitely remember a colder night."

"I wish I had never listened to your question," cried Leithin. "Now I cannot rest until I have found the answer."

So, even though she was angry, Leithin set out again the next morning, and this time she flew all the way to Assaroe, the farthest of all the places to which she had journeyed in search of an answer, and a great distance for a bird as old as she. There, she perched on a rock overlooking the pool where the salmon gathered and waited until she saw a mighty silver fish come to the surface to feed in the shadow of the rocks.

"Are you Goll, the wise and mighty Salmon of Assaroe?" Leithin called.

The salmon put his head out of the water, and she saw that he was indeed half-blind, for one of his eyes was missing and the other was a cloudy gray.

"Who calls to me?" demanded the salmon.

"I am Leithin the eagle, and I have come to ask you a question. But first I must know—how far back does your memory stretch?"

"My memory is a long one," replied the salmon. "I remember the rains that brought the Flood upon the world. I remember the Tuatha Dé Danann, and the Fomorians who came to these shores in the dim time before time. I remember the great one named Lamfadha, who knew the history of the entire Western world, and his son, Fintan the wise, who used to ask questions just like the one you ask."

"Then tell me," begged the eagle, "do you, in all your long lifetime, remember a night as cold as that which came three nights ago? I have already asked the Stag of Ben Bulben and the Blackbird of Clonfert, and neither could tell me."

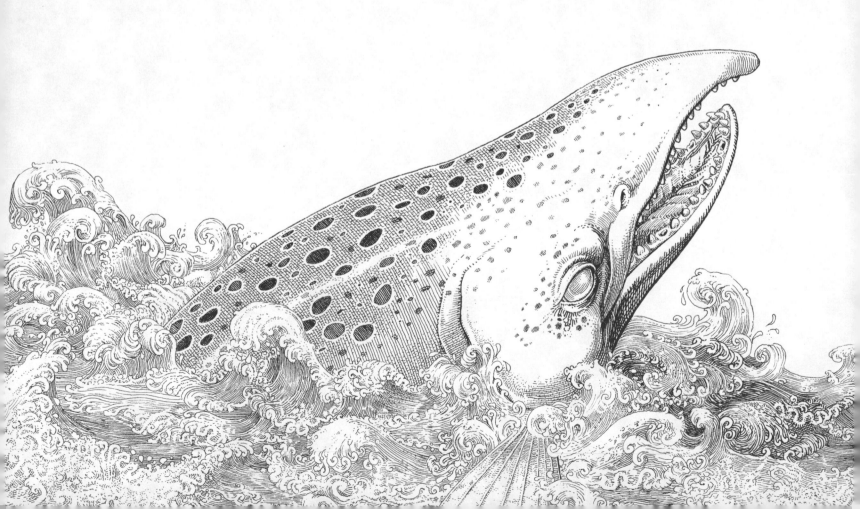

The salmon was silent for a while. Then he spoke: "Once, long ago, I was swimming in this very pool and from it I gave a huge leap. While I was still in the air, the great frost came and froze the water beneath me. As I was floundering on the ice, a crow leaped upon me. If it had not been for my size and weight, he would have carried me off and eaten me, but instead he could take only my eye. The hot blood from my wound fell on the ice and melted it, so that as the crow and I struggled, the ice gave way beneath us and I escaped. I am certain, Leithin, that this was the coldest night in all the ages that I have been alive."

Leithin thanked the old salmon, praising his wisdom and knowledge. But before she could fly away, Goll called up to her, "Was this question your own, or was it another who sent you all these long miles to ask me?"

"Why, it was one of my own nestlings," answered Leithin, "and a cold and weary time I have had of it since then."

"I can see that," replied the ancient salmon, "but it was no nestling who asked this of you."

"What do you mean?" said Leithin.

"There are many things that I have learned in my long life," answered Goll, "and of this I am certain. The bird who asked this question is the Crow of Achill. He has become so weak and frail with age that the only way he can get food is to hide in the nests of other birds. Did you not wonder how this nestling, only just hatched, knew of my brothers and myself? I fear you have been tricked, Leithin, just like many others who have fallen victim to the ancient crow. For this is the very same bird that took the eye from my head on the coldest night of all."

Then Leithin, suddenly fearful for her nestlings, cried out her thanks to the salmon and flew home as fast as she could. There, just as Goll had predicted, she found her nest empty and the old crow long since flown away to seek other foolish birds to rob.

And though Leithin flew to every part of the land for days afterward and heard many tales of his trickery from others, she never again saw the Crow of Achill.

The DEEP, DEEP WELL

This story comes from the great French saga of Reynard the Fox, collected and written down during the Middle Ages.

If there's one thing you can be sure about in the entire world, it's that the old rascal Reynard the Fox is always hungry. Every day he patrols the woods and fields, looking for prey. Every evening he lies in wait around the farms, hoping to catch an unwary hen or a juicy rat.

One day he found himself by a really big farm, with a big wall around it and tall gates to keep him out. But that didn't bother Reynard. He soon found a crack in the wall and crept through. He hid in a big barn until night fell and the full moon rose high in the sky, and then out came Reynard, sniffing around for his next dinner.

It didn't take him long to find where the hens were kept, and without a sound he crept up until he was right next to them—and that was the end of the sleeping hens! Two he ate right away, and a third he tossed over his shoulder in a sack. Then he crept back to his hiding place to rest.

After such a good meal, Reynard soon felt terribly thirsty. As it happened, in the middle of the farmyard was a deep, deep well, with two buckets that could be raised and lowered into the depths to draw up the water.

Reynard rested his paws on the edge of the wellhead and looked down. There he could see the moon like a big piece of cheese, and he could see another fox! Reynard thought it was his own dear wife, Hermeline, and he called out to her: "Hey, Hermeline! What are you doing down there, and how did the moon get down there too?"

When he got no answer, Reynard leaned even farther out, shouting to the fox in the well. The next instant, he lost his footing and fell down and down, deeper and deeper, until he hit the water with a great splash.

Too late, Reynard realized that the fox had not been Hermeline—it had been his own reflection! Now he was stuck. No amount of scrabbling at the walls got him any closer to the top. The water was cold as ice, and Reynard's teeth began to chatter. He climbed into the bucket, hanging just above the water, and sat there shivering.

Now it happened that Isengrim the Wolf was also out hunting that night, and he too came to the farm. Being bigger and stronger than Reynard, he didn't bother looking for a way in but jumped over the wall and into the farmyard. There he made short work of a young lamb and was about to leave, when he heard a hoarse voice calling from the well, "Help! Let me out!"

Curious, Isengrim went to the wellhead and peered deep, deep down into the darkness. He saw a bit of the moon and the face of another wolf looking up at him—and next to her was Reynard!

Well, Isengrim thought it was his dear wife, Hersent, down there and on seeing her with a sly-looking fox, he flew into a rage at once.

"What are you doing down there with that old fox, you trollop?" he shouted.

"Is that you, Isengrim, old friend?" croaked Reynard.

"Who's that?" shouted the wolf.

"It's me—Reynard," replied the fox.

"Reynard! What are you doing down there?"

"Oh, I live here now," answered Reynard, sounding as cheerful as he could. "It's the most magical place, full of good things to eat, warm places to sleep—and it's very safe. I'm so glad I moved here. The world up there was so hard; I never had enough to eat."

"It sounds good," said Isengrim, but he was suspicious of the wily fox.

Reynard took out the hen he had killed earlier and showed it to Isengrim.

"Look," he said, "there are so many hens down here, I will just give you this one. Why don't you come and join me?"

"But how do I get down there?" asked the wolf, drooling at the sight of the hen.

"That's easy enough, old friend. You see that bucket hanging there? All you have to do is get into it and it will bring you down to me."

Eager for the taste of fresh chicken, Isengrim jumped over the wellhead and into the bucket. At once his weight made it drop—and as it went, the other bucket, with Reynard crouching inside it, began to rise.

Halfway between earth and sky the two friends met.

"Hey!" said Isengrim. "Why are you coming up as I go down?"

"That's the rule in the magical world," said Reynard sadly. "Only one person can live down there at a time. I'm giving up my place for a while so that you can enjoy it, old friend."

"Why, thank you," said Isengrim as he sank deeper into the well.

At the top, Reynard jumped out and ran away, while Isengrim found himself sitting in a pool of icy water. Realizing he'd been tricked, he began to howl with rage.

Soon the farmer and his men woke up and came running. They saw the feathers all over the farmyard and the empty henhouse. Then they looked into the well and saw Isengrim.

"It's a wolf!" cried the farmer. "Fetch me my club!"

They pulled the bucket up and beat the wolf to within an inch of his life. When they thought he was quite dead, the farmer and his men left him lying by the well and went back to bed.

Reynard crept out and looked at his friend. Isengrim was only pretending to be dead, but he was too badly hurt to do more than lie still. Reynard helped him to stagger away from the farm and back into the forest. Then he ran off as fast as he could, because he knew that once Isengrim recovered, the wolf would be after him.

After that, you may be sure the two old friends were friends no longer. From that day Isengrim was always trying to get back at Reynard—but those are tales for another time.

HOW ANANSE STOLE All the STORIES

Ananse the Spider is a favorite character in the traditional stories of Ghana.

Ananse the Spider, Ananse the Weaver, Ananse the Trickster was hungry for stories.

He wanted beer in his cup, his finger in the pie, songs in his honor, and all the good things that come to a storyteller when people enjoy his stories. But the problem was that all the stories that ever there were belonged to Nyankopon, the wise Sky God, who looked down upon the earth and so knew the comings and goings of all that had ever happened.

Ananse spun himself up to the Sky Realms on a long thread and saluted the Sky God like an old acquaintance. "Hey, Bright One, I've come shopping. I want to buy all of your stories."

Nyankopon sat unimpressed upon his throne, cloaked in the deep blue of the sky.

"Many people have tried to buy them and failed. My stories don't come cheap. What makes you think you will succeed, little spider?"

"Name your price," said Ananse, cool and confident.

"My price is this: you must bring me four things. I want Onini the Python, Mmoboro the Swarm of Hornets, Osebo the Leopard, and Mmoatia the Spirit of the Trees," commanded Nyankopon.

"Four you want but five you'll get," said Ananse. "I'll go one better and throw in my old mother, Nsia, as well."

"Let it be so," said Nyankopon, bowing his great head in agreement.

Ananse quickly slid down his thread to his own home to tell his wife, Aso, and his

mother, Nsia, about the bargain. But of course he didn't tell his mother the full price he had offered.

Ananse stroked his wife's cheek tenderly. "Wife of mine, honey-sweet, how do we catch Onini the Python?" he asked.

Aso sighed. "Must I be the one to do all the work around here?" she griped. "Go and cut a long stick from the tree and a length of vine and follow me to the river."

Ananse danced off and did as his wife said. Then, down by the river, he and Aso began to argue loudly.

"This stick is definitely longer than he is!" screamed Aso.

"Liar! The python is much longer," cried Ananse.

Their argument rose into the branches above to where Onini the Python lay coiled along a branch that grew over the river.

"What are you two fighting about now?" asked Onini, gliding down.

Ananse explained patiently, "My wife here says that this stick is longer and stronger than you are, and I say it's not."

"Well, there's an easy way to find out," said Aso. "Why doesn't Onini stretch out along the stick and we can see for ourselves?"

"What a good idea, wife! Come down, Onini—don't be shy. I'll make sure that you don't slip off while we measure you by tying you gently with this vine."

Onini the Python crawled down onto the outstretched stick while Ananse drew the vine tightly around the python and the stick.

"Well, look at this!" cried Ananse. "You really are shorter, weaker, and even more stupid than she says!" He looked at Aso and continued, "So that's Onini all tied up." Then he lay back and crossed his legs.

But Aso walloped him over the head. "Get up, you lazy good-for-nothing. That's only a quarter of the price for the stories."

"But, sweet-treasure-of-my-wealth, how shall we catch those fierce hornets without getting stung to death?" Ananse asked.

Aso told him to fetch a gourd and fill it with water and to cut a large banana leaf. "Now go and do as I say, and they shall be yours," she told him.

Ananse positioned himself very carefully and quietly near the branch where the

Mmoboro swarmed in and out of their hanging nest. Then he poured half of the water over the nest and the other half over himself. With the banana leaf over his head, he called out, "Mmoboro, oh, you poor hornets, what a downpour! You'll all be drowned for sure! I've got my banana leaf but you've got no shelter at all. Why don't you come into my gourd and keep dry?"

The Mmoboro streamed from their waterlogged nest, buzzing like angry saws, and flew into the gourd. As soon as they were all inside, Ananse slapped the banana leaf over the hole and trapped them inside.

"Well that's Mmoboro in a jar!" said Ananse, taking his rest.

Aso came into the clearing and found Ananse chewing on a blade of grass. "Get up, you lazybones! That's only half of the payment due," she told him.

"But, marrow-of-my-bone, how shall we catch Osebo the Leopard and not get eaten?" asked Ananse.

Aso told him to dig a pit on the path between the leopard's lair and the water hole and cover it with leaves.

Ananse dug till his many legs were sore. Then he made a framework over the pit, on which he laid leaves and kicked dusty earth over the whole trap to make it invisible. Then he went to where Osebo was sleeping.

From the safety of an overhead branch, Ananse dangled before the leopard's sleep-twitching nose. "Osebo! Osebo!" he called out. "What toothsome food I have for you!"

Osebo sniffed and opened one eye. "Where is the food?"

Ananse swung through the trees, just one claw ahead of the leopard. "It's just over here!"

Osebo saw where Aso was sitting on the path, just ahead of the invisible trap. The leopard licked his lips, gathered himself and sprang forward, but tumbled down into the dark pit.

From deep below, Osebo the Leopard cried, "Let me out! Let me out!"

"If we let you out, you must promise not to eat me or my wife," said Ananse.

"I promise I will not harm you," snarled Osebo.

Then Ananse and Aso bent and lowered a springy branch into the pit with a vine hanging from it.

"We are weak and you are heavy, Osebo. You must tie the vine around your tail and the tree will help you out."

Osebo tied the vine around his tail and shot up into the sky, where he dangled, clawing and snarling.

Ananse threw himself down, worn out by all his work. "Well, that's Osebo on a stick!"

But Aso interrupted him. "Wretched one, you can't rest now, the price is only three-quarters won."

"Queen-of-my-heart, how shall we catch Mmoatia the Tree Spirit? She's slippery as an eel and fine as smoke."

Aso told him to fetch a piece of wood and carve a doll with his knife. So Ananse worked with his knife and carved a life-size, lifelike doll. Then he set it down near where the tree spirits played in a green-shadowed clearing. In front of the doll Aso placed a bowl of yams, and then she poured a gourd of tree resin over the doll.

Hiding in the bushes, they saw Mmoatia gliding down out of the trees, a green shadow with a crown of leaves upon her head. She stopped when she saw the doll.

"I am pleased that you have brought me this offering," she said to the doll, thinking it was a human being who had come to give her a gift.

The doll, however, said nothing.

"You may give me the yams now!" said Mmoatia, extending a shady hand.

The doll's arms stayed firmly by its sides.

Mmoatia lost her temper at this disrespect. "You will regret not giving me this offering!" And she raised her arm and slapped the doll's cheek.

The doll did not make a sound, so Mmoatia brought down her other hand and slapped the arrogant doll on the other cheek. The tree resin glued both Mmoatia's hands to the doll so she could not slip back into the invisible world.

"Well, that's Mmoatia all stuck!" breathed Ananse, lying down to rest.

Aso glared at him, her legs akimbo. "Now tell me, great bargainer, how will you get these captives up to the Sky Realms of Nyankopon? If you think I'm going to carry them all, you can think again!"

"Calm your heart, peace-of-my-rest, I've already thought of that! My mother, Nsia, spins the strongest webs of all spiders. I shall ask for her help."

Away went Ananse to his mother. Ananse the Trickster, what-a-good-boy, apple-of-her-eye, pride-of-her-heart, gave his old mother a kiss. "Mother, I'm going on a visit to the Sky Realms with some gifts for my old friend, Nyankopon. What do you say to a visit with him? You've not had a vacation for so long that I thought you would love to come with me."

Nsia bustled about, getting ready for her visit. "What shall I pack?"

"Nothing, best-mother-in-all-the-world. Nyankopon is a great king who will provide everything for his honored guests. We need only carry the gifts that I've brought for him."

So Nsia spun a strong web and loaded her burden upon her shoulders, carrying Onini all trussed up, Mmoboro in a jar, Osebo on a stick, and Mmoatia all stuck.

Up to the shining realms of Nyankopon went Ananse with his mother on the strong thread that she spun.

"Hey, Shining One, I brought you the payment I promised," cried Ananse. "Give me your stories."

The Sky God looked at Onini all trussed up, Mmoboro in a jar, Osebo on a stick, and Mmoatia all stuck. "Very impressive, Ananse! How in all the world did you capture these most tricky animals?"

Without waiting for an answer, Nyankopon threw back his head and laughed. Then he called the other gods to witness Ananse's triumph. "My friends, many have come begging for my stories, but no one has ever been able to pay the price. See what treasures Ananse has brought! And he brings a special gift beyond the price." Nyankopon took the hand of Nsia. "You shall be my guest of honor and sit by my side when your son tells the stories I shall give to him, and all shall praise you through him."

Nsia blushed and shuffled her feet and kissed Ananse for bringing her to a place of honor among the gods.

And so Nyankopon gave Ananse all his stories. Now it is to Ananse, Snatcher of Legends, Lord of all Liars, Spinner of Stories, to whom all beings pay respect when stories are told. Everyone, that is, except Aso, who said to her husband when he came home, "Only you could sell your own mother for a bunch of stories!"

The AUTHORS and ARTIST

John and Caitlín Matthews

Rare sightings of John Matthews, the great brown bear, have been reported all over Europe and the United States. During the winter he hibernates in a deep book-lined cave and tells stories of King Arthur. In the summer months, he may be found aboard various pirate ships or spying on the fairy folk, collecting stories for his fantastic books.

Caitlín Matthews moves between the salt waters of the sea and the fresh waters of the upland rivers. Always recognizable by her singing, this elusive salmon makes long research trips to the Well of Hazels, absorbing the wisdom of ancient Britain and Ireland and writing down their stories. Catch her by the tail, and she may tell your fortune or give you advice fit for a princess.

Occasionally John makes a pact with Caitlín, agreeing not to eat her, and together they tell fascinating trickster tales and stories of magical creatures.

Tomislav Tomić

Tomislav Tomić is a renowned artisan-beaver. Totally dedicated to creating beautiful illustrations, during the day Tomislav can usually be found in his studio in Zagreb, Croatia, working away, drawing the magical stories of wizards and tricksters. In the evening Tomislav returns to his burrow; he and his lovely wife have two tiny twin beavers to look after, so they are always very, very busy.